***Disclaimer: This is a work of fiction.** Names, characters, businesses, places, events and incidents are either the products of the author's imagination or used in a fictitious manner. Any resemblance to actual persons, living or dead, or actual events is purely coincidental.*

Copyright 2016 by Guardian Publishing Group - All rights reserved.

All rights Reserved. No part of this publication or the information in it may be quoted from or reproduced in any form by means such as printing, scanning, photocopying or otherwise without prior written permission of the copyright holder.

Table of Contents

Chapter 1 3
Chapter 2 15
Chapter 3 26
Chapter 4 37
Chapter 5 49
Chapter 6 61
Chapter 7 73
Chapter 8 84
Chapter 9 96
Chapter 10 108
Chapter 11 119
Chapter 12 131
Chapter 13 142
Chapter 14 155
Chapter 15 166
Chapter 16 178
Chapter 17 190
Chapter 18 201

Chapter 1

Heather rubbed her hands together and smiled at the street outside. It was almost Memorial Day and her spirits couldn't have been higher.

"Are you ready?" Jung asked, beside her. He had his apron on and a grin which was broader than hers.

Everyone in Hillside was happier at this time of year. She glanced around at the Parisian-styled interior of her donut store and sighed. Coffee cups steamed, people chatted and munched on delicious treats.

Now, this was her kind of atmosphere.

"I'm ready," she replied.

Jung wiggled his eyebrows at her and she chuckled.

"Well? Hurry it up, boss. We've got donuts to create... and eat."

"Definitely eat," Heather replied.

"Save for me," Angelica called out from behind the register. She had notoriously good hearing when it came to sweets. She zipped up her cheeky grin and served a customer with a kind one instead.

"All right," Heather said, and clapped once. Dave, her daring doggy survivor, sat up straighter. He'd been a little jumpy after the accident, but had resumed his usual inquisitive and cute dog behavior. Thank goodness for that.

Heather walked towards the office, tailed by Dave and Jung. She opened the office door, let Dave through to his doggy bed, then closed up again and strode into her bakery's kitchen.

"So, what's today's special?"

"It's going to blow your mind, Jung. And your taste buds."

"I'm supposed to be on a diet."

Heather rolled her eyes at him. "You work in a donut shop. Your diet has officially become glaze and sugar." She tied on her own apron, a double bow at the front so it would stick in place, then bent to get a silver bowl. "Besides, you are what you eat. I am ninety-eight percent sure I am an entirely sugar-based lifeform. Throw in a few sprinkles."

Jung fetched the flour and brought it to her. He was used to the procedure by now.

"Speaking of sprinkles," Heather said, tapping her chin, she paused, then clicked her fingers. "I've got it! The perfect donut for Memorial Day."

"And the wedding season," Ken said, busting through the doors. He was the newest addition at Donut Delights.

"Shush you, I can't concentrate on that now," she replied. She really couldn't. Every time she thought of tying the knot to the most eligible and handsome detective in Hillside, her stomach tied knots of its own.

She fanned her face and puffed her cheeks out. She had to get it together. Not every marriage was doomed to end in divorce. Just because her first had failed didn't mean this one would.

She clapped again, to enthuse herself this time. "Bring me the sprinkles, please. That big tub of them over there."

"What are we making?" Jung asked, cocking his head to the side.

"American Dream Donuts. Perfectly baked donuts, cakey and divine, double dipped in snowy white glaze with bright red stripes and stars right across 'em."

"Wow," Ken and Jung said, in unison.

"Please, call me Heather," she quipped.

Ken rubbed his hands and stepped closer. "Heather, I'm

8

sorry I'm late. I had a few errands to run for my, uh, for my grandmother and –"

Heather waved away his excuse. "It's really fine. We have Angelica at the front, and Maricela working the coffee machine. Just call ahead next time, if you can." Heather had never been in the business of bossing her employees around, even though she was the 'boss'.

Still Ken gave her another sheepish smile. His cheeks had colored, as well.

"Where were we?" Heather asked, then spied the tub of sprinkles. "Ah!" She snatched it up and rattled it at her two in. I'll be right back." Heather hurried out of the kitchen and into her office, ripping at the apron and succeeding in tangling the knots even more.

Dave sat up and yawned.

She ripped her apron off at last and threw it into the corner. It flopped onto Dave's head and he wriggled it off.

Heather whipped out her phone and answered without looking at the caller ID.

"That took a while," Ryan said. Even now, his deep voice gave her butterflies.

Goodness, she was over forty. She wasn't accustomed to this teenage lovey feeling in her gut.

"What can I do for you?" Heather asked, straightening her silk blouse.

"You sound busy," Ryan replied.

"Oh, you could say that. You know, the usual, creating in the –"

"I'm going to tell you something, Heather, because I respect and love you. I want you to hear what I have to say without flipping out, okay?"

"Whoa, okay. What's this about? You're not leaving me, are you? Because that would suck. I've already created a series of donuts for the reception. Something Old, Something Borrowed, you get the idea." That was a total babble fest. Her nerves had forced her brain to the back, and had taken her mouth hostage.

"It's about Eva," Ryan said, clearing his throat.

"Eva?" Heather frowned. Eva hadn't been in yet this morning, which was strange for her. "What about her?"

"She's in Hillside Regional hospital," Ryan said, delivering another snippet. Did he think breaking up the news would make it easier to handle?

"Why?"

"Eva Schneider was found this morning outside her home. She'd been hit over the head with a blunt object," he said, as if reading from a police report.

Heather hung up and hurried to the door, clicking her fingers for Dave to follow.

Chapter 2

Heather rested her hand on Eva's forearm, stroking her soft skin with her thumb. The old lady was in a coma, breathing slowly, with tubes trailing in and out of her. Machines beeped in the background, the IV bag was half full.

"Well," Heather murmured, "this is not how I expected my day to turn out." Dave sat on the floor beside her chair, behaving himself best he could. The nurses had allowed him to come in with her, even though it was supposed to be strictly forbidden.

A lot of the residents in Hillside had heard about what she'd done for Verna Dixon and respected her for it.

Amy barged into the private room, hair ruffled, with a pair of pumps hanging from her fingers. She slipped around on the polished linoleum, her stockings giving her about as much grip as a slug in a mud slide.

"I came as soon as I heard," she said, and dropped the pumps to the floor. She slipped into them and walked over. "I can't believe it. Eva."

"The doctors say they have no idea when she'll come out of the coma." Heather sighed.

"How did this even happen? I don't get it. Who would want to hurt Eva? I mean, it's Eva for heaven's sakes. She's a total angel."

"I know right?" Heather let go of her longtime customer and friend, and rose to speak with Amy. "I don't know who or why but –"

"But you intend on finding out," Amy finished.

"Precisely. I'm just glad she's alive, that the killer, attacker, whatever, didn't manage to finish the job." Ack, the 'job' was a pretty crass term to use.

"Have you spoken to Ryan, yet?"

"No, and I don't plan to. I know what he'll say if he finds out I want to investigate this," Heather replied. "And I don't want him to know I'm doing it until I have all the evidence to present to him." She smoothed her hair and squared her shoulders. "I have to take this on myself."

"But –"

"If it were anyone else, I'd let it go. Ryan said that I shouldn't get involved in this kind of stuff from now on." Heather glanced around at the warm walls and the painting of a sunflower hanging from one of them. "But this isn't just anyone. This is Eva, for heaven's sakes."

"I'll help in whatever way I can," Amy replied. "But where do you even start?"

Heather wrinkled her nose. That was, truly, a dilemma. No one hated Eva. She was a harmless old lady with a penchant for sugary sweet donuts and bitter coffee.

"I'll have to check out Eva's home and Hillside Manor. I know she was supposed to visit Soupy there yesterday."

"Soupy? Sounds like a character out of a kid's show." Amy put up a goofy smile. "Well, hello thar keeds," she said.

Heather chuckled softly. Amy always knew how to cheer her up. "Soupy was one of Eva's old friends. An elderly gentleman, she called him. She didn't give me much detail other than that."

"Ooooo, mysterious," Amy said. "I think you and I should get together at Dos Chicos to talk about this."

"I agree," Heather said. "I guess there's nothing more I can do here. I just wanted Eva to know she was loved."

"I thought I'd find you here," Ryan said, striding through the door, professional in his uniform. He didn't reach over and grab

20

Heather for a hug. Instead, he took out his notepad.

"I'll see you tonight," Amy said, with a wave, then moseyed out of the hospital room, making eyes at the back of the detective's head.

Heather ignored her bestie and focused on her fiancé instead. "Sorry I hung up. I just wanted to get here to check –"

"That's fine," Ryan replied, and clicked his ballpoint. "I – uh, I need to ask you a few questions, Heather."

"About what? The flower arrangements? If you really want the roses we can do the roses, just as long as they're long-stemmed and white. Otherwise it's no deal," she said, lowering her voice.

She wasn't sure why. It wasn't like Eva would sit up and glare at her for making too much noise. Boy, that would be creepy.

"No, not the flower arrangements," Ryan said, blinking one, two, three times.

They had discussed flower arrangements at length, after all.

"Oh," she said, then glanced at Eva.

"It's come to my attention that you spoke with Eva yesterday," Ryan said.

"Yes, I did. I speak to Eva every day. You know that, Ryan, she's a regular at Donut Delights," Heather said, and raised an eyebrow. Did he really think she was a suspect in this?

"Did Eva give you any indication that something was wrong?"

"No, not at all. She was her usual sunny self. Ryan, what's going on here? I'm not a suspect, surely? I have an alibi. I was in plain sight in the shop the entire morning."

"Eva wasn't attacked this morning," her fiancé replied. "She was attacked last night."

"And you think I had something to do with it?" Heather folded her arms this time. Her own fiancé thought she was a suspect in the case. Nice.

"I didn't say that. Heather, you know I have to follow all my leads," Ryan said, reaching out to grasp her hand for the first time since entering the room.

"I have to get back to the shop," Heather said, stepping out of reach. "I was in the middle of creating a new donut."

She strode past him before he could say a word, Dave trotting along at her heels. She wasn't angry, but disappointed. Ryan had to know that she would never do anything to harm Eva.

And if Shepherd was determined to follow the wrong leads, investigate silly avenues, then Heather would have to correct him.

She glanced down at her dog. "Dave, consider this investigation under way."

Chapter 3

Soupy's room was decorated with photographs of his family, his son wearing a clown costume, and his wife laughing at their wedding. Cute pictures that Soupy had taken years ago.

"My son's a lawyer now, y'know. He's the best lawyer in the whole state," Soupy said, puffing out his chest with pride.

"I'd like to meet him some day," Heather replied, and smiled. Soupy had an easy attitude. The tufts of hair above each ear gave him a bit of comedic look.

The old man's expressive features crumpled. "You won't.

He never comes to visit me. Just pays the bills and carries on with his hotshot life. Wife died years ago, so I never get to see much family."

Heather restrained a grimace. Poor guy hardly got visitors. Good thing he had a friend like Eva to pop in and pay him a visit.

"Soupy, I'm here to ask about –"

"Soupy! Ha! You wanna know how I got that name?"

She'd assumed at birth, by a pair of particularly cruel parents. Who named their kid Soupy? Seriously.

"Do tell," Heather said, and sat back. She crossed her legs and kept her eye on Dave.

Ever since the accident he'd been in a particularly boisterous frame of mind. This very moment he snuffled around at the base of Soupy's bed, snapping up the leftover crumbs of the old man's brunch. He wiggled his doggy butt and slipped beneath it.

"I served in a soup kitchen, long ago. It was how I met the wife. She was homeless and came in every day round about lunch time for soup. They had other stuff there too, like mash and veg, but she always came for my soup." Soupy sighed and looked out the window at the clear skies. "Soupy, she used to say, Soupy, you're my hero."

Heather chewed the inside of her cheek. She couldn't imagine what it must've been like to be homeless. This man was clearly a saint.

"Soupy, thanks for sharing that with me."

Dave barked underneath the bed, bounced around.

"Stop that, Dave!"

"Don't mind him. I like the noise. Good to hear something other than one of them nurses talking about lunch or pills. Or dinner or pills. Or Mr. Petrakis, please sit still while we adjust the bed. Like I can't adjust the bed myself." Soupy harrumphed and folded his arms.

"Soupy," Heather began.

"Or how about, Mr. Petrakis, get back to bed, it's past curfew." Soupy sat up straighter, the tufts of hair on either side of his hair, swishing from the sudden movement. He leaned to one side and yelled towards the door. "I'm a grown man! I can sleep when I wanna sleep, not when you tell me."

"Soupy, I –"

"You hear me! Don't pretend like you don't hear me," Soupy growled. He shook a fist, and his cheeks went red as two ripe plum tomatoes. "They ignore me, you know, but I know that they know."

"Soupy," Heather said, firmly. "I wanted to ask if Eva came to see you yesterday."

Soupy didn't speak for a while, but at the mention of Eva, all color drained from his cheeks. He flopped back against the cushion. "Nope. Never came to visit. Aint seen her in a week. Nope."

Clearly, that wasn't true. Heather frowned. "You can tell me the truth, Soupy. I don't think you hit her."

"I don't care what you think!" Soupy snapped, and turned his back to her. He stared out the window, and pulled the thin blankets up to his chin. He stuck his lips out in a pout.

Dave barked again and hustled out from under the bed, holding a half-eaten donut in his mouth. A donut that looked a lot like an American Pie she'd created in her shop.

"What the –?" Heather reached for it.

Dave gobbled it up before she got the chance. Trust Dave to eat the evidence.

"Soupy," Heather said.

"Get outta here," Soupy snapped, and pulled the blankets even higher, brushing them past his ears to cover the tufty grey hair above them.

Heather gave it up for a bad job.

She rose and strode out of the room, then glanced both ways. There weren't any caretakers or nurses in sight. Not a one. She needed to double check whether Eva had actually come to visit Soupy or not.

And find out why he'd lie if she had.

A commotion at the end of the hall drew her attention, and she patted her thigh for Dave to follow. They hurried towards the noise, then paused at the intersection. Heather peered around the corner, then snapped back out of sight.

Ryan was here!

He'd come to question suspects and if he saw her he'd be furious. She wasn't supposed to investigate, after all, he'd made that amply clear on several occasions.

Guilt beset her, but she pushed it down. For heaven's sakes, what could she do?

This was Eva. She couldn't let this lie.

assistants. "These are going to add a fireworks effect. A true celebration in the mouth."

"We could do red, white and blue sprinkles for some of them," Ken suggested. "That would make them even more appropriate."

"That's a fantastic idea," Heather said. "Let's start with the multicolored for now, though. The sprinkles will go in the batter and on the glaze after the donuts have been dipped, as well."

Heather's phone rang in her pocket, and she patted her apron down, cursing the double bow.

"You two make a basic donut dough recipe with the sprinkles

Heather hurried in the opposite direction, back the way she'd come. Perhaps she could ask Soupy's neighbor if they'd seen Eva around. The numbers on the doors around his looked familiar.

Warm light spilled from a room two doors down from Soupy's, and a familiar fragrance. A comforting scent.

Heather knocked once and entered. "Leila," she said.

The elderly woman, Heather's grandmother's oldest friend, sat up and smiled. "Heather, dear, what a wonderful surprise. I only expected you to visit again on Friday."

"This is not social call, I'm afraid," Heather replied. "I assume you've heard about Eva?"

Leila nodded gravely. "I'll do whatever I can to help."

"Thank you," she said. "Leila, you didn't by chance see Eva around here yesterday, did you?"

Leila tapped her bottom lip with a gnarled index finger. Her eyes lit up. "As a matter of fact I did. I believe she came to visit Soupy Petraski."

Chapter 4

Heather stood behind the counter, with Angelica at her side, serving customers with a smile. She tried her best to be genuine, but today was difficult.

"You okay, boss?" Angelica asked.

"What's this boss, business?" Heather rolled her eyes. "I'm Heather, remember?" Her assistants loved to tease her about her insistence on not being referred to as the boss. But then, they loved her for it at the same time and Heather was never truly irritated with them for the joke.

"Heatherrrr," Angelica said, rolling out the 'r' and winking. "You distracted today?"

"I won't lie, I've got a lot on my mind." Heather bent to get a box for a woman's order of American Dream donuts, the red, white and blue sprinkle kind. She clipped the box into the right shape, then placed three of the treats inside and handed it over.

"Why?" Angelica asked, after the front of the counter had cleared. She peered down at the array of donuts, and counted on her fingers.

They'd need to restock before lunch, which was their most popular hour.

"Because I can't get Eva off my mind," Heather replied, and pointed to the empty spot by the front window. Sun streamed through and landed on the back of the wrought iron chair. That was Eva's place.

She could almost picture her sitting there, drinking her coffee and munching on a American Dream Donut.

"You should take the day off, go do your investigate." Angelica said, in halting English.

"I'm tempted," Heather replied, then scratched the backs of her arms. "But I need to think this over first. Once again, the truth is not as easy to find as it should be."

Soupy's lie had set her off kilter. He seemed a nice man, a little bit eccentric, but then which resident of Hillside Manor wasn't?

Someone tapped Heather on the shoulder, and she jumped. She turned and was met with Ken's concerned face, his brows drawn down at the sides.

"Ken?" Heather asked.

"May I speak to you for a second? In the office?" He bit his lip and looked past her, at Eva's empty table. "If it's not too much trouble."

"Of course not, no trouble at all. You've got this, right Angie?"

"If you trust me with donuts, yes," she said, then gave a mock evil laugh and stroked the surface of the glass counter.

Heather chuckled. Ken was deadpan.

Whoops, she'd better have a chat with him before he burst into tears.

Heather walked Ken through to the office, and eyed Dave on his portable doggy bed in the corner. He was fast asleep, snoring as he was wont to do, with all four of his paws in the air.

No one could say her dog didn't have character.

Somber Ken actually cracked a smile at the sight of him.

Heather shut the door and directed Ken to the poufy chair in front of her desk. She valued comfort above everything else. The French décor was gorgeous, but would count for nothing if people's butts got sore just lookin' at it.

She circled to her side of the desk, sat down, and then laid her forearms on the dark wood. "What can I do for you, Ken?"

Ken gulped. "I had to talk to you about this, before you found out another way."

Dave flicked his paws in the air, gave a small yowl in his sleep.

"Talk to me about what?" Heather could barely stand the anticipation.

"It's about Eva," Ken said.

"What about her?"

"I visited her yesterday afternoon, you know, to deliver her usual donuts. I think I was the last person to see her before the attack. I'm scared," Ken said, blinking profusely, "I'm scared that the cops will find out I was there and think I had something to do with it."

Heather studied her employee, trying to read him like an open book. And one could never judge a book by its cover. What if this conversation was Ken's cover?

No, no, she refused to think that Ken, her employee, the faithful assistant and kind soul, would have anything to do with Eva's attack.

"Ken, if you had nothing to do with the attack, then there's nothing to fear. After all, the police only go on evidence and if there's no evidence that you hurt anybody, then there's no reason to worry."

Her assistant fidgeted with the cuffs of his shirt. "I just —"

Knuckles rapped against the office door. They both jumped this time, and Dave flipped onto his belly in a quick-as-lightning move to rival a Kung Fu fighter. He yapped once, then settled back into the cushion.

"Come in," Heather called out.

Ryan Shepherd poked his head around the door. "Am I interrupting something?"

"Well, actually —"

Ken shook his head to stop her, suddenly white as fine ground flour.

"I guess not," she said, instead. "How can I help you?" She used her professional tone, because she was still a little angry with him for questioning her.

"Actually, I didn't come to speak with you," Ryan replied, and had the grace to look sheepish about it. He'd tried calling her last night during her dinner with Amy at Dos Chicos, but she'd ignored the call.

"Oh?"

"Yes, I came to question Ken." Ryan tapped his shirt pocket, where his notepad and pen rested against his heart.

Ken went from flour to colorless fondant white. "I – uh – I. Okay," he managed, at last.

"You two can chat in my office," Heather said, rising from her seat. "Just don't touch anything, and for heaven's sake, nobody give Dave a donut. He's gained far too much weight, snapping at scraps."

Ryan nodded and gave Dave a warm smile, but Ken was about as responsive as a fish gone belly up. Or Dave gone belly up for that matter, paws waggling in the air.

Heather walked from the office, a new sense of determination brewing in her belly. It was sleuthin' time.

Chapter 5

Eva's house was more of a quaint cottage than a house, it poked from the concrete in the quiet suburb, where the grass was kept neat and no dogs were allowed.

Dave was the current exception. He stood beside Heather, sniffing at the sidewalk in search of crumbs.

"There are no donuts here, Dave. And that's a terrible habit, by the way. I refuse to endorse it," Heather scolded, wiggling his leash, lightly.

Her dog wasn't used to wearing leashes, but when he did, he always took it with aplomb.

"You'd better behave yourself," Heather whispered. She eyed the house next to Eva's, where another retiree watered his plants with his lips pursed, eyes narrowed and gaze focused on snuffling Dave.

Heather squared her shoulders and marched up the short gravel path which led to Eva's front door. Years ago, when Eva had first become her good friend, she'd given Heather a key for her house, in case of emergency.

Heather slipped it out of her pocket, inserted it into the door and it opened up.

She was bathed in a musky scent of rose petals. It was the same perfume Eva wore, though Eva insisted it was a powder rather than a perfume. A blusher she'd had from before the Great War, as she put it.

Heather hurried inside and through to the living room. She let go of Dave's leash and began the search.

The paisley sofa was clear of blood spots or a mess, but then Eva might not have been attacked in the living room. Ryan hadn't mentioned where the attack had been. Surely the police would've cordoned off the house if the crime had occurred inside?

Heather scratched her temple and walked through to the kitchen. It was empty of evidence too. No threatening notes, no angry messages on the answering machine, nothin.

"Oh boy," Heather murmured. She scanned the kitchen again and something itched at the back of her mind. A missing item? She couldn't quite place it.

She'd been to Eva's house before, but it wasn't as if she'd memorized the interior.

Heather's phone vibrated in her pocket – on silent in case anyone was around to hear it during sleuthin' time. She brought it out and answered.

"This is Heather from Donut Delights."

"And this is Amy from your best friend. We're calling with regards to the lack of contact you've had with us of late. Do you have a complaint to lodge?" Amy was cheeky at the best of times, and a little snarky at the worst.

"Oh poo, what nonsense are you talking this time, Ames."

"I'm talking me, you, dinner tonight. But let's do my place so we can munch on popcorn and watch Beaches."

"I take it I'll be bringing the tissues." Heather and Amy watched beaches together at least once a year, as a reminder of many things, including the value of their friendship. And because crying was cathartic.

"Are you all right?"

"I'm fine. I haven't heard from Ryan since the start of the case. I kind of understand, but it's difficult to plan a wedding without him in the mix," Heather said. It came out in a blurt of emotion, because she'd been holding it in for quite a while.

"Where are you?" Amy asked. "You're breaking up."

Heather pulled the phone from her ear and checked the signal. Only one bar. "Ames, I'll meet you at your house tonight, we'll talk then, all right?"

"Right! Love ya byeeeeee," Amy sang, then clicked off.

Heather chuckled and slipped the phone back into the front pocket of her jeans. At least she had that to look forward to. She strode down the short hall, cream walls of course, and entered Eva's pristine bedroom.

Eva was a total neat freak in the best way. A picture of her late husband hung on the wall opposite the foot of the bed, probably so Eva could wake up to his face each morning, and the bedspread was white decorated with curling pink roses.

Heather smiled softly, but it faded a second later. Nothing here either. No glaring anomalies or clues. She checked under the bed and found an empty suitcase, covered in a thin layer of dust.

A bark rang out from the front porch.

Shoot! She'd totally forgotten about Dave.

Heather barged out of the bedroom and rattled down the hall to the front door. She hurried onto the front porch, just as Dave's cute hiney wiggled out of sight around the corner of the cottage.

"Dave!" Heather hissed, shutting the front door behind her, and sticking the key back in her pocket. "Dave, come back here."

The neighbor next door had increased the level of disdain and the angle of his eyebrows by at least 45 degrees.

Oh boy, she had to get out of here quick. It wouldn't do to have Ryan called in for her snooping around.

Heather dashed down the front steps and around the side of the house.

A cat sat atop the trash cans, arranged neatly beside the back door. It meowed, rose onto its tippy-paws and flicked its tail at Dave.

This, in turn, drove Dave crazy. He barked and hopped up and down on the spot, turned in a circle, then made a mad dash for the cans.

The cat realized its time was up. It leapt off the cans and scooted towards a tree at the end of the yard.

Dave couldn't change direction quick enough, he skidded into the trash cans and knocked them flat. The lids burst open and garbage spilled onto the grass.

"Oh no," Heather groaned, then froze.

What was that?

She hurried over to the cans, ignoring Dave's barking at the base of the tree at the end of the yard. She stepped over an empty pie dish and gasped.

A scrunched up Donut Delights box lay before her, half open, spilling American Pie donuts all over the grass.

What did this mean?

Chapter 6

"So the donuts were in the trash," Amy said, "what's the big deal?" She had her feet up on the sofa, a donut in one hand and popcorn in the other.

When they did a junk food night it was always a debauchery.

"Firstly, my donuts never deserve to be in the trash," Heather side, licking icing off the tip of her finger. "And secondly, because Ken was supposed to deliver those donuts. I don't get it. If he'd delivered them as he said he did, without any problems, then why weren't they in Eva's kitchen? Why were they in the trash?"

"Maybe the attacker saw the donuts and –" Amy trailed off and wriggled her nose, then munched down some popcorn.

"And what? Trashed them because he didn't like donuts? It doesn't add up. Besides," Heather said, with a laden sigh, "there was absolutely no evidence of a break-in. I couldn't even tell where the attack happened."

"You'd think the cops would've checked the trash cans for evidence," Amy replied, gesturing with her donut. "That's shoddy police work, I tell you."

"I don't know, I just don't know."

"Speaking of the police," Amy said.

Heather sighed and shifted the plate on her lap. She grabbed her glass of diet soda and slurped some down, in an effort to prepare for Amy's questions.

"What about them?"

"What's going on with Ryan?" Amy asked. She siphoned down the last of the popcorn and placed the donut on her own plate, which she'd positioned on the coffee table. She readjusted herself, in the typical 'I'm about to get the gossip' manner.

Bright eyed and bushy tailed.

"I don't know what'd going on with him, either. He's so distant lately." Heather rubbed her hands together. "I know I should be understanding, but I've got our wedding to plan and he seems disinterested in it."

"Married to the job?"

"Maybe," Heather replied. "Or maybe he's avoiding me because I'm a suspect in the case and he's afraid they'll take him off it if he gets too close."

"A suspect? That's ridiculous. Wouldn't they automatically take him off it if you were involved, anyway?"

"I don't know," Heather replied, eyeing the credits from their movies. They'd definitely had a good old cry fest. Tissues littered the sofas. "I just wish he'd call and let me know what's going on."

Her phone rang as if she'd activated it by telepathy. They both stared at it, wide-eyed.

Heather chuckled and picked it up, then answered. "Heather Janke, donut maker extraordinaire."

"Miss Janke, I'm calling from Hillside Manor," a woman said, in nasal tones.

"Oh? How can I help?" This was strange. The last place she'd expect to hear from on a relaxed Friday night.

"One of your residents is having a bit of trouble. He's asked for you directly."

"Who is it?"

"Mr. Petraski. He's been yelling all night about being followed and keeps trying to leave his room. It's past visiting hours, but we really think a visit from a family member or a friend would help him right now."

"Of course," Heather replied. "I'll be there in a ten minutes."

She hung up and hopped off the couch.

"What's happened?"

Heather wriggled her eyebrows at Amy. "The plot has thickened. You coming?"

"You bet your bakery I am."

*

Soupy sat straight as a rod in his bed. The nurses had left after Heather arrived, but even her presence – which he'd requested – did nothing to calm the old man.

"Soupy, what's going on?" Heather asked.

Amy hovered by the door, trying and failing to look insignificant. Her beautiful blond friend was anything but insignificant.

Soupy ignored her, however, and focused on Heather's face. "I had to call you. I had to."

"Calm down, it's going to be all right." Heather strode to the seat next to his bed and sank into it. "Why don't you start from the beginning? Talk me through what happened this evening."

"I was in bed, reading," Soupy replied, gesturing to the thick book on his bedside table – Lord of The Rings. "I was at a particularly good part too, when I heard this noise out in the hall.

Like someone trying to break a window."

Heather nodded. "And then what happened."

"Well, I want to check the source o' the commotion. And I saw this shadow thing, this shadow right outside the window across from my room. Nearly jumped right outta my skin," Soupy said, then shivered and gripped the thin bedsheets. "I'm tellin ya, Heather, someone's after me."

Heather tried to keep the doubt from her expression. She failed terribly.

"You don't gotta believe me. Just tellin' you, if something happens to me, you know why."

"Why?" Heather asked.

"Because I'm next. They got poor, old Eva and I'm next. There's a killer on the loose!"

Heather soothed Soupy as best she could, but he didn't settle. They called for the nurses to bring a glass of water, which he promptly threw back at them because they'd 'poisoned' it.

Heather and Amy left a few moments after that, sprayed in water and slightly miserable for it.

"He seems crazy one second and normal the next," Amy whispered.

"That's what I thought too. But it wouldn't hurt to check out the window, see if there might be any interference." Heather replied.

They hurried around to the outside and checked for marks and scratches, but there were none. Except for a single print on the ground. It was rather big, a man's shoe.

"That could be from anywhere though," Heather said, glancing around at the darkened gardens, scanning with the flashlight from her smartphone. "I bet there are gardeners that work out here."

"I bet." Amy said.

But both women shared a freaked out look, before heading back inside.

"Hey," Heather said, "would you like to sleepover tonight?"

Amy nodded mutely.

Whether Soupy had seen a dark shape or not, it had scared Heather enough not to want an empty house that night.

Chapter 7

"This is the second time I've eaten at Dos Chicos this week," Heather said, unable to contain the grin. Overeating Mexican food was one of her favorite past times. Donuts were the other.

"I take it you're not complaining," Ryan replied.

He'd sent her a message that morning and invited her to dinner, and she'd gladly accepted, clearly since she was seated across from him with a plate of steaming enchiladas in front of her.

"I'm glad we did this," Heather said. She twirled the engagement ring on her finger, and they both looked at it. "I was starting to worry I'd never hear from you again. You've been really distant lately."

There, she'd said it. She'd broached the topic and now she probably sounded far too desperate for a woman her age.

But for heaven's sake! He was as closed off a man as any she'd met.

Ryan nodded slowly, dipping his quesadilla in the salsa pot and taking a big bite. He chewed and chewed and chewed.

Heather sniffed, waiting for his answer.

Ryan finally finished his mouthful and cleared his throat. "I know I've been distant. I'm sorry about that." He reached across the table and squeezed her hand. "And I know there's still wedding planning to be done and I really do want to be a big part of that, but I had to keep my distance."

Heather cut into her enchilada, bit off a piece and chewed at length.

He squirmed as much as she had, and she couldn't help a tiny smile. Served him right for making her stress about their relationship.

She was good at keeping it together, years of experience and all that, but that didn't mean she'd enjoyed the whole 'silent treatment' from a grown man. Who happened to be investigating one of her oldest friend's attacks.

"Why did you have to keep your distance?" Heather asked, and balanced the tines of her fork on the side of her plate.

"Because you were a suspect in the case," Ryan replied. He puffed out his cheeks and let out a slow breath. "I know, I know. It might seem crazy to you but I had to do this for my job. I wanted to keep a neutral perspective. And I obviously never thought you attacked Eva, but the other officer couldn't know that."

"So, I take it that you've ruled me out if we're having dinner," Heather replied.

"Yes, I've ruled you out." Ryan tucked into his quesadillas again. After a few minutes of eating, on both their parts, with the music in the restaurant drifting between them, curling in their ears, Ryan smiled and grasped her hand again. "I've missed you. I hope my silence hasn't put a dent in your enthusiasm for our wedding. I really do want to spend the rest of my life with you."

"And I do with you."

It was good to take a night off from sleuthing, and from worrying about Dave's bathroom habits. Another quirk after his accident. He needed the bathroom twenty times a night at least. Okay, probably not as much as that, but that was what it felt like.

She'd dropped him off at Amy's for the night.

"How are things at the shop?" Ryan asked, pushing his empty plate aside for the waiter to collect.

"Oh, they're good. I've brought out a new donut, the American Dream. It's perfect for Memorial Day, but, ugh, things just aren't the same without Eva hanging around."

Ryan grimaced. "I understand. And I'm sorry about that, I really am. Have the doctors contacted you about her condition?"

"No, but I called Hillside Regional and berated the receptionist until she put me through to one." Heather chuckled, but then her mirth died. "The doc says there's been no change in her condition."

"She'll come out of it, don't worry. Soon you'll have Eva back in the shop, telling her stories." Ryan took both her hands this time, and rested his thumb on her engagement ring. "I promise, I'm doing everything I can to get to the bottom of this."

Heather resisted the urge to tell him she was in the process of doing the same. If that wasn't a sure fire way to ruin the evening, then what was?

"Do you have any idea what she was hit with?" Heather asked, puting on her best wide-eyed innocent look. "For the purpose of telling the doctors I mean. Perhaps they could treat her better if they knew."

Ryan narrowed his eyes. He wasn't fooled. "We haven't found the weapon yet." At least he'd told her.

That meant it was still out there, maybe still with the attacker. Another clue.

"Heather, I hope I don't have to warn you not to investigate this. You know that this is police work and getting involved could potentially –"

"I know, I know, you don't have to tell me twice." She beamed at him. "I just wish I could help somehow."

Ryan nodded. "The only way you can help is by telling me if you hear anything or spot any suspicious behavior. Is that clear Heather Janke?"

She stuck out her tongue. "Now you're last naming me?"

"Is that clear," he repeated, deepening his tone. It was half-joke, half-serious.

"All right, all right. It's clear. Clear as glaze. Clear as crystal. Clear as glycerin. Clear as colorless molasses. Clear as –"

"I get it, I get it," Ryan said, raising his hands and chuckling.

It was nice to be in his company again. Now that the tension had broken, she could relax and rifle through bridal magazines without a care.

"What's say you and I have a coffee?" Ryan asked, raising a hand to summon the waiter.

"Sure, but we'll have to make it quick. I can only imagine how many times Dave has peed on Amy's floor by now."

"Oh," Ryan said, pulling a face. "And she has those white carpets in her living room too."

"Right?" Heather laughed.

Chapter 8

Heather eyed Eva's empty window-side seat again, squishing her lips to one side, then the other.

It was a bright Monday morning, and Donut Delights was abuzz with the usual crowd of donut lovers and coffee connoisseurs. Families, friend, groups of old ladies, businessmen. There was such a diverse range of people in the bakery and she loved every second of it.

But it all felt a little empty without Eva.

Ryan might be in charge of the case, and she'd probably suffer guilt for her constant sleuthin, but she wouldn't let this one go until it was solved. Simple as that.

And she only had one lead left.

Maricela and Jung had the counter today, and they worked great as a team, serving up donuts, ringing up orders, handing out coffees.

Angelica was on leave.

And Ken, well, he was in the kitchen, rustling up another batch of Cinnamon Roast Toasty Donuts, and American Dreams in red, white and blue sprinkles.

This was her chance.

"I'll be back in a bit," she said, to the two at the front.

"Whatever ya say boss," Jung replied, with a wave.

Maricela laughed and mimicked him. They got on well, as did all the people in the shop. The place had the perfect atmosphere for comradery, and Heather was proud of that.

She walked through to the kitchen, paused and let the door swing shut behind her.

It didn't make much noise, but Ken still jumped and turned to her, spraying a cupful of sprinkles across the counter.

"Oh, boss, sorry! I didn't mean to mess."

"And I didn't mean to frighten you," Heather replied.

Ken hurried to clean off the sprinkles, but Heather strode over and stopped him with a light touch to the shoulder. He jerked around, as if she'd electrocuted him.

"There's no use crying over spilled sprinkles. Ken, are you all right?"

He swiped sweat off his brow. "I – I'm fine," he said.

"You seem awfully distracted lately."

"I guess I'm a little bit on edge. I don't know if Jung told you, but I don't have the best history with the cops, and the whole Eva thing has brought a lot of my old fears back."

Old fears? No, Jung definitely hadn't told her anything along those lines.

"Ken, I'm always here to talk. Which brings me to why I came to see you," she said, her gazing flicking to the spilled sprinkles. It looked like a party on the kitchen counter. She resisted the urge to swipe a few for casual chewing.

"I'll answer any question you have," Ken said, and wiped his hands down the front of his apron. He had a bit of flour on it, which was very unlike Ken.

All her assistants were neat bakers. Ken hardly messed a drop of an ingredient. He had to be nervous if he'd spilled any flour.

"Ken, I went to Eva's house, just to check it out, you know?" Heather glanced over her shoulder. The coast was clear, no Ryan to burst in and bust her mid-sleuth.

"Okay," Ken replied, and bit the inside of his cheek, so it hollowed inwards.

"I found a Donuts Delights box in the trash can. It was the delivery of donuts you were supposed to bring to her that afternoon." Heather tucked her hands behind her back and clasped them together. "I can't understand why they would be there. Did you dump them in the trash?"

Ken was pale again. This entire affair had taken a toll on his nervous system.

"No, I would never put any of your donuts in the trash. I love baking, I love donuts. I love Donut Delights."

"Then, well, um," Heather trailed off, to collect her thoughts. She circled the counter and rested her back against the massive steel fridge in one corner. "Do you have any idea how they might have ended up there?"

"I do," Ken whispered. "I know I should've told you this before, but I was scared. I'm really scared the police will try to arrest me. Before I worked here, I had a rough life and the police, well they weren't my biggest fan, let's put it that way."

Heather tilted her head to the side. "So how did the donuts end up in Eva's trash?" She respected Ken's privacy. Even if he'd done something wrong prior to his employment at Donut Delights, it really wasn't her business.

There was a difference between sleuthing and prying into another human being's personal life.

"Here's what happened," Ken said, and straightened. "I arrived to deliver the donuts to Eva, but when I got there she was already out front, watering her garden. I left the donuts on the front porch and said goodbye."

"Sounds normal enough."

"Exactly, but when I got the car and looked back…" Ken swallowed, and his eyes went round as buttons. "When I looked back, there was someone else walking towards the house."

"Who?" Heather asked, curiosity poking holes in her patience. "Who was it?"

"It was Gary Larkin," Ken said. "You know, the guy from the Chamber of Commerce?"

It was Heather's turn to go wide-eyed. They stared at each other in shock.

Gary Larkin. He was the guy who'd dated a killer. His career had been ruined after Sheila's demise.

"Oh boy, that's not good to hear. But what would Gary Larkin want with Eva? They barely knew each other. In fact, I'm not sure if they'd even met before." Heather wriggled her nose, allowing her poor eyes to return to their normal size.

"I have no idea, but he was walking like he meant business. Swinging those big arms back and forth like pendulums."

"Pendulums," Heather repeated, for the sake of saying something, anything at all.

This threw yet another lead into the case. Was it a lead or a monkey wrench?

"Thanks, Ken," Heather said, and patted her employee on the shoulder. "You get back to work, and don't worry about the cops.

It's like I said, if you didn't do it, they can't arrest you. Am I right?"

Ken gave a weak smile and turned to clean up the spilled sprinkles.

Chapter 9

Gary Larkin had fallen from grace since the whole 'girlfriend and secret affair guilty of murder' thing. The Chamber of Commerce didn't look kindly on those types of interactions.

His offices certainly weren't on Main Street anymore, but on a road which looked more like a back alley.

The brick-faced two story building was peppered with graffiti, and an overflowing dumpster was tucked against it on one side.

Heather wrinkled her nose. Dave didn't snuffle at all. He had a taste for donuts, not for trash, and his attitude was distinctly uppity.

He looked at her as if to say 'Why have you brought me here, woman?'

"We have to question him, Dave, he's our only lead right now."

Apart from Ken, who she didn't want to consider because he was, well, he was Ken, for heaven's sake.

Heather strode to the front door of the building, and stood on the concrete stoop, tapping her heel. Was this a good idea? What if Gary went to the cops and told them she'd been sticking her nose where he thought it didn't belong?

Ryan would be irate for going against his request.

Ah well, life was for living and Heather was too curious to worry about that, now.

Dave whined.

"Curiosity did bring the cat back, you know," she said, and nudged him with the toe of her pump.

She pressed the buzzer beside the door, waited for the responding 'bzzzz', then entered.

A receptionist sat behind a wooden desk, painting her nails and flipping through a magazine.

She licked her thumb, flipped a page and continued reading, not bothering to glance up.

Heather wrinkled her brow, not that the rude woman noticed.

She stepped forward and peered at the magazine.

Oh, an article about Amber Heard breaking it off with Johnny Depp. No wonder she was oblivious to the world around her.

"Excuse me," Heather said, politely as she could manage. She had a lot of stress with the wedding coming up, so it took every ounce of her patience not to slap the woman over the head with her Johnny Depp article.

The receptionist painted another nail. Didn't answer her.

"Hello!" Heather raised her voice, then rapped her knuckles on the wood of the desk. Dave yapped.

"Yeah, I heard you," the receptionist said, without looking up from the article.

"I'm here to see Gary Larkin." Seriously, this was the rudest person she'd encountered. And that said a lot. She'd dealt with the mother of a beauty queen, who also happened to have been a cold-blooded murderer.

"Get in line," the receptionist replied. Her name tag read Tina Tonks.

Heather glanced around the empty reception area, decorated as it was with brown sofas and a moisture stain on the ceiling.

"What line? There is no line."

"Then make one," Tina Tonks replied, flipping the page.

A full two page centerfold of Johnny Depp himself, in a panama hat with a gold earring.

"Tina," Heather said, "if you don't make eye contact with me sometime soon, I might let my dog have a wee in here. He's got an exceptionally weak bladder."

Dave whined on cue.

"What do I care?" Tina asked, a rhetorical question in monotone, because clearly Tina didn't care at all.

"Are those knock-off Gucci shoes?" Heather asked. The implication was clear. Especially when Dave whined again.

Finally, Tina Tonks looked up and flicked her bright blue hair back from her eyes. She had smeared on fuchsia lipstick and some of it had transferred to her teeth.

"What do you want?" Tina asked, at last.

"To. See. Gary. Larkin." Heather said, between gritted teeth.

"He's not in at the moment."

"Oh, when will he be back?" Heather asked, and Dave bumped against her leg. Boy, he really did have to go to the bathroom, after all.

"I have no idea, lady, but I doubt he'll take your appointment. He's stopped taking appointments lately. Been real moody too." Tina Tonks took a slurp of her coffee. "Yeah, he's a pretty rude guy."

Look who's talking.

"Great," Heather said, "thanks." That was belated and she didn't mean it, but her sense of courtesy demanded she make that kind of statement.

Tina Tonks was under no such obligation. She shrugged and returned to her magazine. "Door's open if you wanna leave."

If she wanted to leave? This was hardly a welcome atmosphere. She'd have been hard-pressed to stay.

Heather didn't say goodbye. She strode out of the front door and out into the dingy street, holding Dave's leash tightly.

What a horrible woman.

Heather eyed the building and hummed. Perhaps she'd better stay after all. She could probably walk right past Tina without her looking up from Johnny and

Amber. Shoot, she should've thought of that before she'd left.

There might be evidence in Gary's office.

It alarmed her that Gary Larkin had been angrier of late. A rude guy. What did that mean?

Heather marched back to the front door and extended a finger to press the buzzer again.

"Heather?"

Uh oh. Caught red-handed.

"Heather, what are you doing here?"

She turned to face Ryan. He stood a short way off, beside his police car, with his arms folded. Dapper in his police uniform, wearing an expression which was anything but.

"You're investigating," Ryan said. "I asked you not to. Don't you realize you're jeopardizing evidence in this case?"

"Ryan, I –"

"I don't want to hear the excuses," Ryan replied, holding out his palm. "Now, come on, I'll take you and Dave home. Enough is enough."

Why couldn't he understand that she had to do this? It was Eva. Eva had been hurt and she felt more involved this time around.

"Heather –"

"I'm coming," she snapped, then tugged at Dave's leash. Together, they walked to the police car, his leash clicking and her stomach rumbling with nerves.

Chapter 10

"He didn't talk at all?" Amy asked, folding her arms across her chest.

"Not one bit. The entire ride home he was as silent as the grave. Even when I tried to explain that this is personal. I mean, you get it right?" Heather beat the egg whites by hand, because it was good to have something to do that was physically draining.

"Yeah, I get it," Amy replied, and glugged back a mouthful of iced coffee. Decaf at this time of night or they'd never get to bed.

Heather wasn't much for girly sleepovers, especially at her age, but lately she'd needed the moral support, and Amy had been happy to oblige. What were best friends for?

"I don't want to jeopardize his case, but I won't let the cops handle it and mess it up."

"I sure hope you didn't say that to him," Amy said, and swiped a bit of batter from the other bowl.

Heather had decided a treat was in order, and that treat was her specialty Lemon Meringue Donuts.

"No," Heather replied. "I didn't want to make his cheeks even redder than they already were. He looked about ready to pop a valve. I can understand why. He did ask me to butt out."

"So why haven't you?"

"Do you remember what happened with Gustavo? Angelica and Maricela's cousin?"

"Yeah, I remember," Amy said, nodding.

"They thought it was self-defense and that he was a bad kid, but I knew the truth all along. I'm not some all-knowing sage, but the police aren't infallible. I'd rather handle a personal matter like this, myself." Heather worked the egg white, and her arm ached. She relished that sensation, a reminder that she was here, she was real and her feelings mattered.

Her ex-husband hadn't thought so. She feared that Ryan didn't either.

"As long as you take Dave with you wherever you go," Amy said.

The dog perked up at the mention of his name, tipping his head to one side.

"He ruined my carpets the last time I had to babysit." Amy cracked up laughing in spite of the situation. "I'm just kidding Dave, you're always welcome at my house." She sauntered over to the naughty pup and cooed at him, then petted the soft patch between his ears.

"Are you going to help me with these?" Heather asked. "Or use Dave as a shield for your laziness?" She brandished the whisk at her lifelong friend and waggled it. Bits of egg white flopped off and splattered the tiles.

"She's onto me," Amy said, in a stage whisper.

An hour later, they were in the living room, snacking on donuts which were positively moan-worthy. If Heather did say so herself.

"Sleuthing and Donuts. Your two talents," Amy pronounced.

"I'm starting to wonder about the sleuthing. I can't figure this case out. There's a total lack of clues."

Amy sat up straighter, licking meringue and sugary dust off her fingertips. "Ooo, sounding board time, let's hear your theories, I love it. The mystery is too intriguing."

"All right, so," Heather said, squishing around on the sofa, so she could better discuss the matter at hand. "Ken delivered the donuts to Eva's house on the afternoon before the attack."

"Right, got it," Amy said.

"And he said he dropped the donuts off on the front porch."

"But you found them in the trash." Amy took a bite of donut and groaned. "And no one in their right mind would trash these babies."

"He said, that he saw Gary Larkin walking up to the house, but he didn't see any altercation between Gary and Eva." Heather rubbed her lips together. "I can't get hold of Gary Larkin and I don't have any other suspects."

"Except for Soupy," Amy said, pointing with a meringue-tipped finger. "He lied to you and said Eva didn't visit, when she did. And he made up that story about someone watching him. I bet he did it."

"I don't know about that. I can't draw that kind of conclusion yet." Heather readjusted herself again, but no amount of moving and shaking would jolt lose any new ideas.

She was pretty much stumped.

"There aren't enough clues," Heather whispered. "Maybe Ryan's right. Maybe I should just let him do his job and butt out of it."

"Could you really do that?"

Heather thought back to the sunny days in Donut Delights.

The meaningful chats with Eva and how supportive she'd been about Ryan and the engagement in general. She couldn't picture not having Eva Schneider at her wedding.

"No. I couldn't." Heather said, at last. "I just wish I had more information. The only option I have left is to do some snooping around Gary."

"We could Google him. Find out what he's been up to lately."

"I already did. Just a few complaints about unethical behavior, and he's been booted from the Chamber of Commerce. Stuff we already knew about."

"Ouch," Amy said, "that had to sting."

"He brought that upon himself," Heather said, sagely. She stifled a yawn on the back of her hand, then checked her watch. "Ack, it's getting way too late. We'd better catch a nap. I can't be pooped at work tomorrow. We've got another batch of American Dream Donuts to make."

"They're popular?"

"Oh yeah. The closer we get to Memorial Day the faster those suckers sell right out." Heather rose from the sofa and swept Amy into a quick hug.

They'd meant to plan the wedding tonight, or at least get a start on it, but the case was a total sidetrack. Heather hurried upstairs with Dave in tow, and got ready for bed.

She settled onto her mattress a short while later, thoughts of Eva's attacker and the lack of clues sweeping through her mind, over and over again. It was another hour before she finally fell into an uneasy sleep.

Chapter 11

Heather groaned and rolled over in bed, snuggling deeper into the duvet. The air-conditioning was on full blast in her bedroom.

Dave yapped at the end of the bed.

She ignored him and drifted in and out of her dreams.

He barked again.

"For heaven's sake, Dave, keep it down," she groaned, then cracked an eyelid to check the time. It was barely past three in the morning.

This dog, goodness, he was like a pregnant woman. He needed the bathroom at all hours of the night. Ah well, at least he didn't have hormonal problems and a bad temperament.

Bang, bang, bang!

Heather opened both eyes and frowned, scanning her darkened bedroom. What was that noise? Dave barked again.

A thrill of alarm ran up Heather's spine, and she bolted upright, swung her legs over the edge of the bed, then clicked on her bedside lamp.

Honey yellow light flooded her bedroom. Dave was on the floor by her bedroom door, scratching frantically to get outta there.

"What is it?" She wondered out loud, and tilted her head to listen again.

Bang, bang, bang!

That was from downstairs.

The door to her bedroom swung inwards, and Amy stood there, wearing her blanket like a shroud. "I think there's someone at the door."

"At the door? It's three in the morning!"

"You're telling me," Amy replied, stifling a yawn.

Dave scooted past her, bark on repeat, and scrabbled down the stairs, heading right for the entrance hall.

"Oh boy," Heather murmured. "What could this be about?" She slipped out of bed, grabbed her loose cotton robe off its hook behind the door, and then put it on.

Together, Amy and Heather dashed down the stairs and to the front door. Dave hopped up and down on the spot, barking furiously.

"Shouldn't we ask who's there before we open?" Amy asked.

"That's what peepholes are for," Heather said, pointing at the lens in the top board of the door.

She stood on tiptoe and peered out, while Amy hovered in her peripheral vision, still firmly tucked into her blankie.

"Oh my," Heather whispered.

"What, who is it?"

"It's Soupy," she replied.

Heather unlocked the door and opened up for the elderly gentleman. He was wild-eyed, his hair sticking straight out above his ears, as if he'd been electrified. He gibbered and wrung his hands.

"I had to come."

"Soupy, what are you doing out here?" Heather was positive Hillside Manor didn't let its residents wander, at least not on purpose.

"I had to come," Soupy repeated, rocking back and forth of the balls of his feet. "May I come in?"

"Of course," Heather replied, and stepped back to give him room to enter.

Soupy shuffled inside, and stamped his muddy boots out on the wooden boards in her entrance hall.

"Why are you here, Soupy?" Heather asked, as gently as she could manage.

Dave circled the old man, snorted at his boots, licking and probing with his wet black nose.

"Dave," Heather hissed.

He ignored her and carried on with his investigation. Apparently, sleuthing ran in the family.

Soupy didn't answer the question, but glanced back at the now closed door, and then met Heather's gaze. He reached into his pocket slowly, fumbled around, and brought out...

A photograph.

He handed it to her, wordlessly.

"What is it?" Amy whispered. Curiosity had finally gotten the better of her. She'd dropped the blanket from her head, and gathered it around her shoulders instead.

Heather gasped. "It's me. Where did this come from?"

"Somebody slipped it under my door an hour ago," Soupy replied, his tone gravelly with fear.

The image showed Heather, sitting at Soupy's bedside, as they spoke about the case. The picture had to have been taken from right outside Soupy's bedroom window.

Heather traced the edges of the photograph, frowning. "What does this mean?"

"It means they're coming for us next," Soupy grunted. "Don't you see? They want us gone. They're angry that Eva didn't die and they want us –"

"Calm yourself, Soupy. Calm, please," Heather said, and grasped his arm. She turned to her best friend. "Ames, will you take Soupy here into the kitchen and brew him up a cup of tea for his nerves?"

"Of course," Amy said, then hooked her arm through Soupy's and guided the old man down the hall. He followed her quietly, shoulders slumped, tailed, of course, by sniffing, tail-waggling Dave.

The poor guy has been through a lot lately.

Heather studied the photo. Was it possible that Eva's attacker had taken this photo? But why?

It was a threat to her. Or was it a threat to Soupy?

Question bundled in her mind, a roiling mass of confusion. She had to solve this case, and fast, because whatever this was, it wasn't a friendly gesture.

Heather hurried upstairs and stowed the picture in the top

drawer of her dresser, for later examination. She picked up her smartphone and dialed the number for Hillside Manor, then reported Soupy's appearance at her house.

He would need to get back to his room that night.

Heather finished the call and traipsed back down the stairs.

Soupy met her in the hall. "I'm not crazy, Heather. Someone is after us."

"I don't think you're crazy."

Soupy nodded, his gaze sharp for once. "I lied about Eva visiting me. She came the afternoon of her murder. She used to bring me donuts. She was such a wonderful woman."

"Why did you lie?" Heather asked.

"I didn't want you to think I hurt her. I was afraid, I –"

The doorbell rang, splitting Soupy's confession open. He looked to the door and then at Heather. "I don't want to go back," he said. "What if I'm next?"

"Don't worry, Soupy, I'm going to get to the bottom of this." Heather said, with confidence she didn't feel.

Chapter 12

Heather sat at one of the tables in Donut Delights and admired the centerpiece, the porcelain vase brimming with flowers. Her stomach was aflutter with nerves in spite of the rumble of happy customers and the amazing aesthetic.

She had a date with Ryan.

She'd asked him to meet with her in the bakery, because it was past time she let him in on a few truths about the case.

Soupy's visit the night before had put a whole new spin on the situation, and the plot was thicker than lumpy custard, right now.

She just couldn't make head nor tails of it.

Ryan bustled into the shop, spotted her and made his way over. His expression was somber. They hadn't talked much since the 'Gary Larkin' incident, and he probably hadn't forgiven her for interfering.

He sat down across from her, and Heather presented him with a donut.

Ryan didn't pick it up, but did take a sip of iced coffee from the glass beside the plate. "Thanks," he said.

"I know you're angry," Heather said.

"I'm not angry, I'm just disappointed."

"Is this what it feels like to be disapproved of by a parent?" Heather scratched at her temple with her nail, then chuckled. "Come on, Ryan, you know I'm not trying to mess up the case."

"Do I?" He asked, and worked his jaw. He sighed, at last. "Okay, I know you're not. I understand why you're doing this, but it's still a big problem for me when you do stuff like this. You understand that, right?"

"Of course," she said. "It was just this case, Ryan. It's personal. It's Eva!"

"I know. I —"

"Wait," Heather said, raising a hand. She reached into her purse and brought out the picture Soupy had given her. She slid it across the table. "I thought you should see this."

Ryan frowned and picked it up. "A picture of you with an old guy? Is this your method of breaking up with me? Because I gotta say, that's an interesting choice for a date."

Heather laughed. "Be serious."

"What is this?" He asked, shifting in the chair.

"I interviewed Soupy a few days ago, about Eva's attack, you know? And last night, someone slipped this picture under his door." Heather poked the image of herself in the face. "He thinks it was the attacker, threatening us."

Ryan digested for a moment, and then picked up his American Dream Donut, bit off a piece of sugary goodness and digested that too.

"I think you need to get an officer at Hillside Manor, to watch over him. Because not only has he been wandering around at night, but he's also afraid, and clearly this is some form of threat."

Ryan gestured with the half-eaten donut, the colorful sprinkles inside caught her eye. "I don't think it will be a problem."

"Great, so you'll –"

"No, I mean I don't think threats will be a problem anymore."

"Why not?" Heather frowned.

"Because we caught Eva's attacker this morning." Ryan said, matter-of-factly.

Heather coughed into her fist. "What? Who was it?"

"A local waitress. We investigated her because she had a vicious argument with Eva the day before the attack. Apparently, she took exception to Eva asking for her meal heated up."

"How do you know it was her?"

"We found a bloodied baseball bat in her possession. We've sent it to the lab for DNA testing, but it's pretty much cut and dry." Ryan rubbed his sugary fingers on a napkin, then dotted the piece of thin paper against his lips. "So, Soupy's not in danger anymore, and you can stop investigating. It's over."

Heather licked her lips. If it was over, then why did she feel so empty?

This didn't make sense. She hadn't heard anything about this waitress or the argument. "Wait, when did you arrest this woman?"

"This morning."

The waitress might've had the chance to slip a picture under Soupy's door, but this still didn't sit right with her. Her sleuth senses were a-tingling and they told her that this wasn't the end.

It was too easy.

The front door opened and Ken strolled in for his shift, wearing a camera around his neck, suspended by a thick strap.

Heather blinked and did a double take. Ryan followed her gaze.

"Heather," he said, and grabbed her hand. "Relax, please, you're seeing signs in everything. I'm beginning to think the upcoming wedding, the cases in the past, all of it seems to be getting to you."

"No, I'm fine," Heather said. But she wasn't truly 'fine' and it had nothing to do with wedding stress or anything else, except for the pure and simple fact that this case wasn't over.

Ken walked to the front and spoke enthusiastically with Angelica, who grinned and chatted back. Her two assistants, getting on as they should.

Heather pursed her lips and wriggled them around.

Since when had Ken taken up photography?

"Heather? Halloo, Earth to Heather." Ryan patted her forearm.

"Oh, sorry. I was somewhere else completely. What's up?" Heather asked.

"I was saying we should get together tonight to plan the wedding. Meet up at a restaurant first, have a little dinner, then have coffee and discuss it." Ryan's face was alight with anticipation. He'd already forgiven her for going against his word, and all he wanted was to spend time with his fiancé.

"Yes," Heather replied, managing a smile. "Yes, that would be wonderful. I'll call Amy and ask her to babysit Dave."

"Oh, I'm sure she'll love that," Ryan chuckled.

Heather laughed with him. The cogs in her brain clicked and turned. Clues in a case, evidence, suspects, but none of it added up to a random waitress attacking an innocent old lady over a cold meal.

There had to be another answer. And Heather would find it.

Chapter 13

Heather stood behind the counter in Donut Delights, and grinned at one of her regulars. She was a teenager, Janice, who came in after soccer practice, on most week days hungry for whatever Donut was new or on special.

"How's life treating you?" Heather asked.

"Great. Loving the soccer," Janice replied, between mouthfuls of donut. "And hey, I still get allowance from the rents, so I get to have donuts every day. It's pretty awesome."

"That *is* awesome," Heather said, and handed over the closed box of donuts which Janice had ordered to go. She was a good kid, always ordered an extra half dozen for her parents.

"Awesome sauce! See ya around, Heather," Janice said, and waved with the donut, then hustled past the queue of hungry customers and out into the boiling heat. An oven-like wind baked the street outside, driving more and more people inside, seeking iced coffees and sweet sustenance.

Heather certainly wouldn't complain about that.

She focused on serving customers, but every now and then a stray thought would creep into her mind. What if Ryan and the cops had apprehended the wrong person? What if Eva was still in danger? Or Soupy for that matter.

She did her best to put up a smile, laugh and be jovial. After a while, her jaw strained from over compensating.

"Uh, boss? You kinda look like a Cheshire cat," Jung said, giving her the side-eye.

"I can't help it," she said, massaging her jaw. "I'm worrying constantly about Eva and if I don't put a super bright smile, the customers might get a frown instead."

"Maybe you should take a break."

"It's good to keep busy," Heather said, by way of explanation. "Besides, I wanted to talk to you about something."

"Sure, what's up?"

The line of customers dwindled at last, and Heather turned to face her assistant head-on. He handed her a cup of coffee before she could get down to business.

"You've seen Ken with the camera, right?" Heather asked.

"Yeah, sure. He told me he's started taking photography

classes. He really wants to get into it."

"I see," Heather said, and slurped down some coffee. The bitter liquid swirled down the back of her throat and sploshed into empty belly. "I see."

"Uh oh, what's this about? You've got that 'Sleuth Gone Wild' look in your eye."

Heather snorted and a bit of coffee sprayed from her nose. She dabbed at it with a handkerchief, eyes watering. "Sleuth Gone Wild?"

"Yes, like you're onto something. Has this got to do with Eva?"

Jung asked, edging closer and lowering his voice.

The door to the bakery slammed open, hard. The interior fell quiet immediately, which was no mean feat, since at least forty people were crammed into the small space.

Gary Larkin stood just inside, glaring directly at Heather.

"And this is where I make a hasty exit," Jung murmured, backing away slowly.

"Traitor," Heather whispered, but she didn't mean it, of course.

Slowly, the buzz of conversation picked up again. People returned to their donuts and chat.

Gary Larkin continued staring as if Heather was his focal point, the center of his universe.

Blegh. That would be the worst place to be.

"Heather Janke," he said, striding between tables, bumping the backs of chairs and ignoring protests from the other customers.

"Well, hello there, Gary. Fancy seeing you here," she said, lightly. She tucked her hands behind her back and gripped her apron strings for support. She truly despised conflict and it was clear that that was exactly what Gary had on his mind.

"As if you haven't done enough," he said, loudly.

A few of the people at tables closest to the front perked up at the insinuation of fresh gossip.

That was one thing about the citizens of Hillside, they sure loved their gossip.

By nightfall, the story of Gary Larkin's appearance in Donut Delights would've been upgraded to a full scale confrontation, police and ambulance called for good measure.

"Is there something I can help you with?" Heather asked, amiably. The best defense was a smile. Always, a smile.

Unless you were attacked and forced into a freezer. Then the best defense was a pack of frozen sausages.

"You can help me by never coming near my offices again. Tina told me what you did."

"I don't know what shocks me more, that Tina remembered or that she even told you. She's not exactly employee of the month," Heather replied. She wasn't snarky, just trying to deal with Gary as best she could.

"Don't get smart with me, woman. I know what you're up to. You're trying to destroy me, again!"

"I didn't destroy you, Gary. I didn't get you kicked off the Chamber of Commerce. You did that all by yourself."

Bad thing to say.

Gary Larkin drew himself up straight and puffed out his chest. "How dare you!" He yelled.

That yell woke up Dave, who'd been curled up in the corner on his velour cushion. He barked at Gary for daring to yell at his beloved mistress.

"How dare you!" Gary yelled.

"Mr. Larkin," Heather said, formally, "I'm afraid I'm going to have to ask you to leave. You're disturbing my customers."

"You horrible, egregious woman!"

"That's not the right use of egregious."

Gary slammed his fists down on the glass counter. A few people yelled in surprise.

And Dave, oh boy, Dave had had enough of Gary's behavior.

He hopped off his cushion and scooted around the counter, growling and barking, a dog possessed. He launched himself at Gary and grabbed hold of the leg of his pants, then tugged with all his might.

The situation quickly devolved.

Gary yelled and spun in circles, Dave growled and ripped the pants, people screamed, others laughed.

"Dave no!" Heather yelled.

But Dave was in no mood for instruction. He ripped, growled and tugged until finally…

Riiiiiip.

Gary's pants tore at the seam.

Thump!

An object dropped to the floor. Heather leaned forward to catch a glimpse of it, just as Gary dropped to pick it up.

A camera. It was a camera.

Gary met Heather's gaze, then turned and fled the bakery.

Chapter 14

Heather sat beside Eva's hospital bed and sighed. She stroked the old lady's wrinkled forehead, thinking back to her stories, and their times chatting together. It'd been great fun and Eva had been a friend whenever Heather needed her.

She had to return that favor.

She couldn't exactly jolt Eva out of her coma – boy that would help solving the crime – but she could continue on the path she'd set off down the minute she'd heard about the attack.

"I'll find out who did this to you," she whispered, "the real attacker."

It was ridiculous. It wasn't as if she had any indication that the waitress Ryan had arrested wasn't the real attacker.

Heather rubbed her hands together and resisted the urge to fetch herself one of those terrible hospital coffees.

Gary Larkin was on her mind, all right. That trick in Donut Delights had brought the police, but when they realized that he was gone, they'd left. The camera. That was what got to her.

He'd been all fury and fire until the camera dropped from his pocket and he *saw* her looking at it. Could he be the one who'd taken the picture?

Could he be Eva's attacker?

The door to the private room swung inwards, and a nurse bustled in, carrying a clipboard and a new IV bag.

"Hi there," she said, "I didn't expect her to have any company today. I can come back another time."

"No, that's all right," Heather said. A light clicked on in the dark recesses of her mind. "Wait a second, what do you mean 'today'? Who else has been visiting with Eva?"

The nurse removed the old IV bag and clipped on the new one, then checked it worked. "What?" She asked, focusing on Heather again. "Oh, no one, really, but there is this sort of funny character who keeps trying to visit her."

"A funny character?" Heather only knew one 'funny character' in Hillside, and he happened to have tufty hair above each ear, and a loose relationship with curfews.

"Yes, we haven't let him through yet. We screen visitors for our patients, as you know, and he refused to provide identification." The nurse sniffed. "I was at the nurse's station near reception when he came in the first time. He kicked up quite a fuss when they wouldn't let him past."

"The first time?"

"Yes, he tried at least two more times. On the last occasion, he tried to sneak right past the reception desk," the nurse replied, walking two fingers in mid-air.

The nurse was in her mid-twenties, with an easy smile and an open, honest face. She'd tied her tight, dark braids back into a ponytail.

"What's your name?" Heather asked.

"Lara," she replied, with a grin.

"I'm Heather Janke," she said, then sucked in a breath. "Lara, could you do me a favor and call the cops?"

"Oh my goodness, what for?"

"I need to talk to one of them. Detective Ryan Shepherd specifically." Heather had left her phone at home. She'd wanted to switch off the outside world during her visit with Eva.

"Of course, I can do that for you. I'll ask them to come down here." Lara's dark brow wrinkled. "This has to do with the unwelcome visitor, I take it?"

"Absolutely."

Lara nodded and hurried out of the room, taking the empty IV bag with her.

Heather was alone with her thoughts again, and her thoughts were particularly cloying. They chased her conscience around in circles.

What if it was Soupy? What if he'd come to attack Eva, to kill her even? No, but Soupy wouldn't do that. He was the scared one, and the picture that'd been taken had been of him and Heather.

But wait, he could've easily asked someone to take the picture of them together, then faked his fear.

Twenty agonizing minutes passed.

Finally, the door to the room opened again, and Ryan strolled in, handsome in his uniform.

She rose, then gave him a tight squeeze.

He held her out at arm's length and searched her face. "What's the matter? Why didn't you answer your cell?"

"Oh, I left it at home. I wanted to be alone with Eva and my thoughts. Turns out that was a good idea."

"Why?"

"You can ask Nurse Lara or any of the receptionists about this, to verify the story, but apparently, there's been a shady character, a man, hanging around the hospital and trying to get into Eva's room." Heather nodded. "I'm sure it's the attacker."

"Heather," Ryan said, then shook his head. "We have Eva's attacker in custody."

"Have you gotten the DNA results back yet?"

"Well, no, but I'm sure that —"

Heather pulled back from her fiancé and folded her arms. She raised her chin and looked down at him. Sort of up and down, since he was taller than her. "Then you can't possibly say that it's definitely her."

"There's evidence —"

"Ryan, I'm not asking you to arrest anyone. Just put a security detail on Eva's room, please. There's clearly somebody sneaking around." She was grasping at straws in her argument. "Ah, it might even be one of your suspect's relatives seeking revenge."

Ryan thought it over for a minute, glanced at Eva, surrounded by tubes and machines and looking awfully small. He nodded, at last. "I'll see to it. But you have to promise me that you won't do any more investigating."

"I wasn't investigating," she replied, innocently.

Ryan grunted, but she still didn't make the promise. How could she when she had yet another lead, one she had to follow through on the minute she left the hospital room.

"Trust me," Ryan said, "the cops have got this under control."

"If you say so." She said it too soft for him to make out.

Chapter 15

"I can't believe we're doing this," Amy said, in another of her classic stage whispers.

They were inside Hillside Manor, after managing to jimmy the window into the hall open, and slip through. Amy had had to hand Dave through the window, which he'd enjoyed, since he loved the attention.

Either way, all three of them were inside, hovering in the hall like cat burglars.

Dave seemed to understand how important this was, because he was quiet for once.

"Remind me why we didn't come during the day?" Amy whispered, checking the coast was clear. Her head swiveled left and right, constantly.

"I want to check out Soupy's room while he's sleeping." Heather sniffed. "I'm beginning to wonder about this place. Security is really lax."

"Well, I highly doubt they expect their residents to go walkies in the middle of the night. Or that anyone would break in to snoop in a pensioner's bedroom."

"This is ludicrous, isn't it?" Heather asked.

Amy shrugged, but the seed of embarrassment was planted.

She'd been absolutely certain that Soupy was the 'funny character' who'd been sneaking around the hospital. His behavior fit that Modus Operandi. He'd lied about Eva visiting him, Dave had found a Donut Delights donut under his bed, and he'd been escaping Hillside Manor with shocking ease.

But now, she wasn't as sure.

What if this was another of her assumptions?

She'd been wrong before.

"Are we doing this? Or do you want to stand in this super spooky hall all night long?" Amy hissed.

"Coming," Heather whispered, and rushed up behind her friend, and Dave, who'd already set off down the hall. "Ames, what if I'm wrong about this? What if I was wrong about this whole thing and I should've spent my time planning the wedding instead of sleuthin'?"

"Don't be so hard on yourself," Amy replied. "I think you've done the right thing. Something about Soupy doesn't feel right and I'm keen to find out what."

"Uh oh, looks like you've got my investigation bug." Heather looped her arm through her friend's and they hurried down the hall together.

Soupy's room was close. They checked the brass numbers on each door. All the lights in the room were off, except for one.

"Shoot," Heather said, "he's awake."

Muffled voices travelled down the hall. Amy and Heather shared a glance.

Who would Soupy be talking to at this hour?

They crept closer, Heather checked on Dave, who kept close to her legs and silent as her could, given that his claws pat, pat, pattered on the linoleum floor.

They stopped just outside Soupy's door, and Heather placed her palm against the cool brass knob. The teak scent of wood, the sweetness of ancient varnish, tickled her nostalgia nerve.

She moved to open, but Amy grabbed her before she could. "Wait," she mouthed. "Listen."

Heather nodded and let go of the handle.

They leaned in and placed their ears against the door. Boy, if Soupy opened it now, wouldn't they look like two ripe bananas standing there, eavesdropping.

"Why do you think I'm here?" A man spoke. A voice that she recognized but couldn't quite place. It was calm and quiet, but there was a grunt to it.

"I don't care. Get out before I call security," Soupy replied, loudly. He was definitely aggravated. "I know who you are. You're the one who's been sendin' them pictures. You hurt Eva."

"Eva. Yes, she was an unfortunate casualty but I had to do that to get what I wanted."

"Get out," Soup repeated.

"I don't think so. You see, Soupy," the man hissed, mocking the nickname, "I've come for my payout and you can believe that I'm going to get it."

Amy and Heather exchanged looks. Payout? Was their money involved in this?

"I have no idea what you're talking about," Soupy grunted. A clatter of plastic and then silence.

"Don't try to call the front desk again. You'll regret it." The man's footsteps travelled back and forth on the floor in Soupy's room. Heavy footsteps.

Dave growled softly. Heather and Amy shushed him, then held their breaths in case the attacker had heard.

But the man, whoever he was, was in the process of a full blown villain rant.

"I've waited months, years for this moment. Building up my strength, creating a plan which couldn't fail. You see, Soupy, my ledger is full, but I've got a lot of red ink in my book."

"Huh?" Soupy was as puzzle as Amy, whose brows had formed two inverted ticks.

"I need to balance the books, Petraski. What don't you get? If I don't, I'll lose more than I earn. Do you understand?" The man asked, and ceased his pacing.

"I understand you're crazy. And I know who you are, I know."

"All the more reason to get rid of you, my good man."

Soupy wouldn't be deterred. "You're that fellow who –"

Dave's growls turned into a sharp yap, and tense silence fell in Soupy's room. Heather had heard enough anyway. She knew exactly who it was in there with Soupy.

Ledgers? Red ink?

The tinkle of glass breaking. Dave lost all self-control and digressed into a yammering dog creature. He scratched at Soupy's door, demanding access.

Heather was happy to oblige. She opened up and rushed in, with Amy hot on her heels.

Soupy looked as if he'd seen a ghost. He clutched the sheets to his chest, blinking in rapid succession. The window was broken, glass had sprayed outwards, but some of it had fallen on Soupy's prized bookshelf.

There was no need to ask which way the attacker had gone.

"Are you all right, Soupy?" Heather asked.

The old man nodded slowly, and swallowed. "I'll live," he replied, "but I don't know for how much longer if you don't catch that guy."

"Who was it?" Amy asked.

Soupy and Heather shared a glance, then answered in unison. "Gary Larkin."

Chapter 16

Heather had left Dave outta this one. The last time she'd taken him for a walk around town hadn't exactly ended in happiness and sunshine. And Amy, well, she had a date night going on.

That was fine.

Heather didn't want anyone else to be involved in this. She was about to cross the line, in a very big way. Her desperation to find the attacker and bring him to justice had boiled down to this moment.

Heather's phone buzzed in her pocket, on silent again. She took it out and checked the caller ID.

Ryan. She didn't answer, but waited for the phone to settle down again.

A message flashed on the screen and she tapped to read it.

Hope you're okay. Very quiet. Missin you. Just wanted to let you know that you were right. The blood on the bat didn't match Eva.

Heather didn't reply.

The message just injected her with more determination to follow through.

She hurried down the street and crept towards Gary Larkin's house. It was a squat one story, brick-faced building with two windows either side of its grey front door. Creepy as could be.

"Maybe this wasn't such a good idea, after all." Heather paused and touched a hand to the phone in her pocket. She could call Ryan and tell him what she knew, but no, that would take too long.

Ryan would need to get a warrant to arrest and question Gary, let alone one to search his house. This was the only way she could get him here, and find what she needed to stop Larkin before he took out his 'ledger anger' on Soupy.

Trust him to use books and accounting to talk about his murderous intent.

Heather crouched down and crept around the back of his house.

Gary's car wasn't in the drive, but that didn't guarantee he wasn't home. Her heart pattered out a rhythm of fear.

"You can do this," she whispered, and squared her shoulders.

She hurried to the back door and tried it, but it was locked up tight, and Heather Janke was no locksmith.

She stepped back with a frown. There had to be a way into the building.

"Oh duh," she said. It didn't matter if anyone saw she'd broken and entered. After they found out why, she'd be off the hook. Wouldn't she?

Heather shrugged and bent to grab a rock nearby, which sat within the border of a dilapidated flower bed, stems wilting from the excessive heat. She lifted it, then froze. A key sparkled up at her from the dark brown soil.

"Bingo." Heather dropped the rock and picked up the key instead, then inserted it into the back door and opened up.

She stepped into the murky kitchen, and rammed her fist against her nose to block the smell. It smelled fishy in here, but worse than that. She didn't click on the kitchen light. Still, the darkness didn't hide the overflowing trash can beside the fridge, or the half-eaten meal still on the table.

Clearly, Larkin wasn't much of a cleaner.

Heather made her way out of the kitchen to begin the search. She entered the living room, tripped over a worn ottoman, and slapped into the beige carpet on all fours.

Ouch.

She grimaced and sat back on her feet, her knees pointing towards the center of the room.

"This was a great idea," she said, and rolled her eyes. At least he didn't have an alarm to kill the mood.

Heather pushed herself up from the floor, and shuffled around in the living room, lifting books, peering between the leaves of a half-dead potted plant, and flicking the thin, filmy curtains back to check the coast was still clear outside.

She bustled out of the living room and walked smack dab into the wall.

Ouch again.

She rubbed the bridge of her nose. Best investigation ever. Seriously, she had to make this her full time job.

Heather stepped back and eyed the wall, then narrowed her eyes. That wasn't a wall, that was a door. It didn't have a handle though. The spot where the knob should've been had been blocked up.

Heather placed her hands against it and pushed.

Nope, not budging.

She pushed harder.

The door creaked and wobbled.

"Let's try this one more time," Heather said. She took two giant steps back, then reassessed her life. She'd broken into a stranger's home – possible killer and boring accountant to boot – and was about to take a running jump at a rather solid door.

Heather rubbed her hands together. "YOLO," she said, then shrugged.

She hurtled towards the door, and hit it broadside.

Crash!

The door burst at the hinges and crashed inwards.

She lost her balance and went right down with it, in a cloud of dust and wood splinters.

Triple ouch.

That was more than enough athletics for one day. If she didn't find the evidence she needed now, she'd call it a day and limp back to Donut Delights to lick her wounds.

Heather looked up, through the clearing dust motes, and gasped.

"Jackpot," she whispered.

The entirety of the wall opposite was covered in photographs of Soupy and Heather, Heather and Ken, Heather and Ryan eating dinner at Dos Chicos, even one of Amy and Heather, eating popcorn and donuts.

A cold chill rand down Heathers' spine, and her skin tried to crawl right off her body.

There was a common denominator in all these photos.

She pushed herself up, not bothering to dust off her jeans and loose shirt. She stumbled over the wreck of the door and stomped to the photo shrine. There was a shelf beside it, which held a mini-statue. A gold award with a plaque which spoke of Gary's service to the Chamber of Commerce. The top end was blunt and spattered with… dried blood.

The image in the center was of Heather and Eva, sitting at Eva's regular table, enjoying coffee and a chat. A huge red cross marred the image.

"It's me," she whispered. "He's after me. It wasn't about Eva after all."

The front door to the house creaked open.

Chapter 17

Heather's heart skipped about twenty beats in a row. Never in her life had the sound of door opening struck as much fear into her mind as it did now.

Larkin was home.

The image of Jack Nicholson in The Shining popped into her head, unbidden. What a great moment to think about that particular movie.

She needed a plan, and she needed out, before Larkin saw the mess that was his secret, Heather-hating shrine room door.

Heather whipped out her cell, unlocked the phone and tapped through to camera. She took twenty photos in the span of a second, thanks to her trembling thumb. Then she retreated to the entrance of the room.

Gary's heavy footsteps rang out in the living room. They headed through to the kitchen and stopped.

"What the –?" He said.

Oh shoot, she'd forgotten to take the key out of the back door and close it.

Heather darted out into the hall, and made for the front door. She slammed into it, scrabbled at the doorknob.

Gary's footsteps stomped towards her.

She turned the knob, then dashed out of the house, down the concrete front steps and dove into the hedge bordering the property.

Heather schooled herself to calm, trying not to tremble. There wasn't a breath of wind, and if Gary walked out and spotted one of the hedge's shivering, he'd know something was up.

She spied through the leaves.

He was on the front porch, all right, with his hand above his brow searching left and right. He eyed the bush and she froze, her pulse racing again, but that gaze moved on, scanning the street.

Gary hovered on the porch for a couple minutes more, then marched back into his house and slammed the door shut behind him.

Heather fumbled with her phone, swiped the screen and clicked through to images. She had a lot of blurry ones, but a few were pretty incriminating. She sent them to Ryan immediately, with the caption: *attack weapon and images found in Gary Larkin's house. I'm here, come quick.*

Heather sweated it out in the bushes – and man, did she hate sweating, it was the least ladylike thing to do, she day dreamed of being back in her kitchen at Donut Delights with her quirky assistants rather than here.

A message made her phone buzz.

Stay hidden. Cops on the way.

Relief shuddered through Heather's body. That was that. Gary Larkin would be arrested and Eva's attacker would meet justice. But why had Gary hated her that much in the first place?

It had to be because of Sheila's death.

He blamed her for it, and for his fall from grace. That made sense. Especially given that the attempted murder weapon was a Chamber of Commerce award. Talk about unpoetic 'justice'.

A couple minutes past, and a terrific roar of anger rang out from the interior of Gary's house. Oh boy, he'd found the broken Heather-hating shrine. He had to know that she'd seen it.

"What if he tries to run?" Heather whispered.

Seconds later, Gary burst out of his front door again and onto the porch, car keys in hand. He stormed down the front stairs and towards the beat up Volvo parked in the drive.

It was now or never, if Heather didn't stop him no one would and he'd get off scot-free.

She tumbled out of the bush with a yell. "Gary!"

He stopped mid-stride, posture rigid. He turned on the spot, slowly, ever so slowly, and faced her. "It was you. You wrecked my house."

"Hardly worse than beating an old lady over the head with a fake trophy," she replied, calling upon the confidence she had inside to face him.

"You don't get to talk to me like that," Gary barked. "You're the one who ruined me, who ruined all of this!"

"I would apologize, Gary, I really would, but Sheila died because she did the wrong thing." Heather sighed and held her phone behind her back, gripping it so hard that the plastic made a crack of protest. "I'm only sad that you decided to follow in her footsteps."

"It wasn't Sheila's fault, it was yours! You took her from me!" Gary yelled, face turning bright red beneath the orange mop of hair on his head.

"I didn't take anything from you. But you tried to take my friend from me."

He stepped towards her, snorting air in and out of his nostrils.

"Don't take a step closer, Gary. I've already called the cops. They're on the way to talk to you now, and if you hurt me, they'll know exactly why and who it was. Understand?" Heather spoke in a clean tones, completely calm, and sirens rang out in the distance to corroborate her claim.

Gary spun towards the noise, then back to her. "I –"

"It's no use, Gary. It's over now. You need to explain this all to the police, and hopefully, if you confess and you change your outlook, you can redeem yourself."

Birds chirped in the trees, a strange offset to their situation.

Gary didn't move a muscle. He was frozen to the spot, gulping air and opening and closing his mouth continuously. "I didn't – I don't –" And then his face crumpled into sorrow.

She had a hard time feeling bad for him.

The police cars pulled up, and officers jumped out, guns at the ready. Gary Larkin sobbed noisily.

"Put your hands above your head!" Ryan yelled, aiming his gun expertly.

Gary did as he was told.

Heather sucked in a gasp which filled her from mouth hole to toes. That had been a close one.

Ah well, all in a day's work. And what a day of work it had been. She couldn't wait to get home and down an entire box of donuts as a reward.

Chapter 18

"And that was it?" Amy asked.

"That was it," Heather replied. "He didn't attack me or anything. I think on some level, Gary had already given up. It's the reason he didn't manage to kill Eva, or why he didn't do away with Soupy when he had the chance."

"But why?" Amy stood beside the counter in Donut Delights, snacking on a Memorial Day Donut.

"Because he had his grand plan, but he wasn't like Sheila. He couldn't go through with it to the extent she had." Heather brushed her hands off on her apron. "He still made the wrong choice though."

"I bet Ryan wasn't too pleased that you put yourself in danger... again."

Heather shook her head mutely. No, Detective Ryan Shepherd definitely hadn't been pleased, but he hadn't been angry either. Just happy that she was safe.

It was a quiet afternoon in the bakery, and almost time to close up for the day. The few patrons left at the tables snacked on their donuts with less chatter than usual. News of Larkin's transgressions had already spread, and a couple of the customers had openly asked Heather about her involvement.

"The wedding is going ahead as planned?" Amy asked, in her usual Amy probe manner. Oh she could be pushy when she wanted to be, but Heather loved that about her bestie.

She truly cared.

"Yes indeed. Except now with the case out of the way, I've got a lot of planning to do." Heather smiled, and her gaze travelled to the empty table at the front of the shop, where dearest Eva should've been seated.

Dave had taken it upon himself to fill that empty gap. He'd curled up in the last sliver of sun on Eva's empty chair, this time with all four paws tucked beneath him.

Ken strolled up to the counter and stopped in front of the register. "Hiya, boss."

"Ken, what are you doing here? I told you to go home early. It's Friday for heaven's sakes," Heather said.

"I had a question for you. I hope you won't think it's too forward."

"Oh?" Heather and Amy exchanged looks. "Sure, what's up?"

Ken gestured to the camera hanging from a strap around in

his neck. "I wondered if you'd let me take some photographs of your donuts. I think it would be a great idea to set up a website for Donut Delights, and since I've been doing a photography course lately…"

Heather clapped her hands, delight building in her chest. "Yes, that would be fantastic. And what an awesome idea."

"Really cool," Amy agreed.

The front door to the bakery opened and Ryan entered, flapping the front of his shirt from the heat. He paused to scratch Dave between the ears, then strode to the front counter, wearing a broad smile.

"Hey, honey," Heather said.

He walked around the counter, gave her a hug, then spun her on the spot and stared into her eyes. "I have some good news and some bad news."

"Oh? Give me the bad news first."

"You can't go out with Amy this evening," Ryan said, "that is, if she'll relinquish you for just one night."

"And why's that?" Heather asked.

Amy arched an eyebrow and clicked her tongue. "Always trying to steal my Heather away."

"Because I wanted to take you out to celebrate," Ryan said, then winked.

"Celebrate what exactly?"

"That's the good news," he replied, then tapped the side of his nose. "You're going to love this."

"Stop, I can't stand the suspense a moment longer," Heather replied. "Tell us."

"I think it would be better for me to show you, rather than to tell you. Wanna close the shop early?" Ryan asked, glancing as the last of the straggling customers traipsed out of the door. "It's a Friday, trust me, you'll love this."

"All right, but only if Amy can come too. And Dave."

"Of course," Ryan said. "Meet me out by the car in five."

The women made short work of tidying and locking up, then piled out of Donut Delights and into the back of Ryan's cruiser.

"I feel like a petty criminal," Amy remarked, and clung to the grill which separated the front of the car from the back.

Dave barked is agreement.

"Keep talkin and I'll take you in for disturbing the peace," Ryan replied, in a tough guy cop voice.

They all chuckled.

Twenty five minutes later they were inside Eva Schneider's hospital room, greeted by the shining face of the woman herself.

"Eva!" Heather rushed towards the bed, and Dave yipped and turned in circles at the sound of her joy.

"Hello, my dears," Eva said, and patted the side of her bed for Heather to take a seat.

She took it gladly and grasped Eva's frail hand in her own. "I'm so glad you're awake."

"Not even coma can keep this old bird down," Eva replied, then laughed, a tinkling note of mirth which lifted the mood in the room, instantly. "I heard you've been up to your usual tactics. Solving crimes. Bringing justice to those who need it."

"Don't encourage her," Ryan said, from the door.

"Oh shush, you," Eva replied, flapping her hands. "If it hadn't been for Heather's superior investigating skills, you'd have the wrong girl in custody right now."

Heather's curiosity gene itched and squirmed at its locus. "Eva, what happened the night you were attacked?"

"Oh my dear, it wasn't the night, it was the day."

They all gathered round to listen, except for Ryan, who'd already heard her testimony and written a report on it.

"It was just after my delivery of donuts had arrived. I was gardening, minding my own business, when Gary Larkin walked up to me and raised this torrid gold trophy thing." Eva broke off and shuddered, delicately. "The next thing I remember, I was waking up in this room."

Heather patted Eva's arm. "It's good to have you back, Eva. Donut Delights has missed you."

"You didn't happen to bring any donuts, did you?" Eva asked, her grey eyebrows dancing around.

Laughter filled the room once more.

THE END

A letter from the Author

To each and every one of my Amazing readers: *I hope you enjoyed this story as much as I enjoyed writing it. Let me know what you think by leaving a review!*

I'll be releasing another installment in two weeks so to stay in the loop (and to get free books and other fancy stuff) [Join my Book club](#).

Stay Curious,

Susan Gillard

CPSIA information can be obtained
at www.ICGtesting.com
Printed in the USA
LVHW081210220319
611422LV00040B/657/P